KID SQUAD

SAVES the World

The Comet of Doom

by John Perritano   Illustrated by Mike Laughead

Calico

An Imprint of Magic Wagon
www.abdopublishing.com

www.abdopublishing.com

Published by Magic Wagon, a division of ABDO, PO Box 398166, Minneapolis,
Minnesota 55439. Copyright © 2015 by Abdo Consulting Group, Inc.
International copyrights reserved in all countries. No part of this book may
be reproduced in any form without written permission from the publisher.
Calico™ is a trademark and logo of Magic Wagon.

Printed in the United States of America, North Mankato, Minnesota.
042014
092014

**THIS BOOK CONTAINS
RECYCLED MATERIALS**

Written by John Perritano
Illustrated by Mike Laughead
Edited by Rochelle Baltzer and Megan M. Gunderson
Cover and interior design by Candice Keimig

Library of Congress Cataloging-in-Publication Data

Perritano, John, author.
 The comet of doom / by John Perritano ; illustrated by Mike
Laughead.
    pages cm. -- (Kid Squad saves the world)
 Summary: Mad scientist Dr. Alowishus Cobalt has used a tractor
beam to alter the course of a comet and aim it at Earth, and it
is up to the Kid Squad--Pi, Athena, Gadget, Tank, and their
trusty cat D-Day to save the world from destruction.
 ISBN 978-1-62402-038-4
1. Comets--Juvenile fiction. 2. Inventions--Juvenile fiction.
3. Scientists--Juvenile fiction. 4. Heroes--Juvenile fiction.
5. Cats--Juvenile fiction. [1. Comets--Fiction. 2. Inventions--
Fiction. 3. Scientists--Fiction. 4. Heroes--Fiction. 5. Cats--
Fiction.] I. Laughead, Mike, illustrator. II. Title.
 PZ7.P43415Co 2014
 813.6--dc23
            2014001049

Table of Contents

Chapter 1
First Sighting

Dr. I.N. Stein loved bologna sandwiches. Each night before going to work, Dr. Stein made himself a triple-decker bologna, lettuce, tomato, banana, and mustard sandwich. There was nothing better in "zee whole wide world," the professor said in his thick German accent.

He washed down his late-night treat with a tall glass of chocolate milk. "It is, what do zee Americans say? *Yummers*. Yes, zee sandwich is very much yummers," he muttered to himself.

Dr. Stein nibbled on his mighty sandwich as he worked alone in his secret laboratory located on a hill deep in the Amazon rain forest in South America.

Dr. Stein loved the jungle. He especially liked listening to the chattering crickets and the squirrel monkeys that swung on vines from tree to tree. He felt at home under the clear, star-filled sky.

Tonight, like most nights, was uneventful. The good doctor sat in front of the world's most super-sensitive computerized telescope and scanned the heavens, measuring the distance of stars and looking at the rings of Saturn. He plotted the paths of asteroids and the orbits of the planets.

As he finished the last of his sandwich, a strange blip appeared. Dr. Stein took a sip of milk, pushed his crazy, fright-wig hair from his eyes, and looked closer.

"It can't be," he said softly to himself. "It is impossible."

But there it was as plain as the spectacles on his wrinkled nose. "It can't be," he said

again, this time much louder and to no one, for Dr. Stein worked alone. "*Nein, nein, nein.* No, no, no. There must be something wrong."

Dr. Stein busily checked his equipment. The computers were still computing. The telescope's eye was still in focus. Yet there it was—a comet, its tail ablaze as it sped toward the sun.

"There should not be zee comet in that area," Dr. Stein said. "Something is, how do you say, *not right*. Yes, something is not right."

The comet, and a very big one at that, was hurling through space amazingly fast. Dr. Stein wrote some figures on a piece of paper and looked up in shock. "*Nein*. No!" he yelled. "It cannot be. It cannot be."

Dr. Stein, one of the smartest men on the planet, had just calculated that the comet was on a collision course with Earth. The answer was the same no matter how many times he checked his math.

"Zee comet will hit Earth in six days," he said. "Then we will all be *kaput*."

Yes, *kaput*. It was not a word Dr. Stein liked to use. It meant wrecked, ruined, see ya later, "zee end."

Where had this comet come from? Dr. Stein didn't seem to know. If anyone knew about comets, it was Dr. Stein. He spent most of his life studying these space travelers. This comet was huge—as long as the island of Manhattan. It should not have appeared out of nowhere. Dr. Stein should have spotted it weeks, if not months ago.

"Comets do not just pop up," he said. "Something is how you say, *fishy*."

Indeed, something was fishy.

"Cobalt!" Dr. Stein yelled. "It is him. I know it! Cobalt has his hand in this. I can feel it in zee bones. That monster. That insane monster."

If Dr. Alowishus Cobalt was involved in this soon-to-be tragedy, it would not have shocked anyone. He was, after all, a mad scientist, perhaps the maddest. Moments later, Dr. Stein realized his worst fears. He heard a bell and looked to his computer. An e-mail appeared in his inbox.

From: Dr. Alowishus Cobalt

To: Professor I.N. Stein

Subject: Comet of Doom

My Dear Ignatius:

By now, you have determined that a comet is on a collision course with Earth. And by now, you have realized that I have something to do with this.

You are very smart, my dear Ignatius. Last week, I completed one of my more, shall I say, gripping inventions—a tractor beam that could snatch a comet from the deep reaches of our solar system and hurl it toward Earth. In six days, Earth will be a smoking cinder. I do apologize.

Of course, there is a way out. The nations of your lovely planet need to give me $200 billion in gold, and you need to give me the Amulator. When I have both in my grubby hands, I will direct the comet away from Earth and back into a harmless orbit around the sun. All will be as it was. If the *world denies my request, well, you are smart enough to know what will happen.*

Go now, Ignatius, and tell the world this tale of doom. You have six days. Six days to save Earth, Ignatius. You and the others laughed at me. Now, I will have the last laugh.

Sincerely,

Dr. Cobalt

¤

Dr. Ignatius Newton Stein slumped in his chair, scratched his gray head, took off his glasses, and then rubbed his weary eyes with both hands.

Six days!

Six days to save the planet.

"What will I do?" he mumbled. "What will I do?"

Chapter 2
Holy Guacamole!

"C'mon Tank," Pi shouted from the stands. "Hit a home run! All we need is a home run."

Tank dug his spikes into the dirt and took two practice swings. With a runner on first, it was the last chance for Copernicus Middle School to win the ball game. The Astronauts were losing 3–2 to the Highlandville Sharks. The Astronauts would win the game if Tank hit one over the fence.

"We're gonna lose," Athena whined as she nervously twirled her curly blonde hair. "I just know it . . . we're gonna lose."

"Shh," Pi said. "Think good thoughts and Tank will smack one over the fence."

Athena thought good thoughts. Pi crossed her fingers and toes just to play it safe. The pitcher for the Sharks went into his windup and let the ball fly. Tank was ready—he was born ready. He watched with the eyes of an eagle as the sphere sped toward him. The ball dipped a little on the wind, but no matter, for Tank was the best hitter the Astronauts had.

Tank stepped into the oncoming pitch and took a mighty swing. The air seemed to shatter as the ball cut through the cloudless sky with the speed of a supersonic missile. Pi and Athena watched in wide-eyed amazement. The ball rocketed over the left field fence, coming to rest with a crash on the hood of a parked car.

"Home run . . . home run!" Athena shouted, shaking Pi. "I knew we'd win the game . . . I knew Tank would hit a home run!"

Pi looked at Athena and rolled her big brown eyes. Twenty minutes later, the three friends were celebrating at the Shake & Stir, which made the best hamburgers in Webster's Corners.

As Pi was about to sample the Shake & Stir's "World Famous" French fries—Athena always ate a veggie burger topped with shredded carrots and hummus—her cell phone buzzed and a special notification appeared. Pi knew it meant trouble.

"We gotta go guys," Pi announced, pushing her dark hair from her face. Tank and Athena looked up in surprise. "Dr. Stein needs us, and it doesn't look good."

¤

Gadget was already at the Kid Squad headquarters when Pi, Athena, and Tank bolted through the door. D-Day, whom Athena had rescued when he was just a kitten, sat on top of a bank of computer screens, lifting his head up ever so slightly as the gang assembled.

"You should have seen Tank smack that ball over the fence to win the game," Athena told Gadget as she walked over to pet D-Day. "It was

13

the most amazing thing I ever saw. I knew he'd hit a homer. I just knew it."

"It was nothin'," Tank said, his face red with embarrassment.

"Any news, Gadget?" Pi interrupted. It was time to focus.

"Not yet," Gadget said, adjusting his wire-rimmed glasses. "Colonel Bragg will be on the holophone call with Dr. Stein. I'm charging up the Amulator and the access pads just in case we have to leave in a hurry."

"Good idea," Pi said. "Something big must be going on if Bragg is joining us."

The holophone crackled to life. There, appearing in a sheet of yellow-green light, were Dr. Stein and Colonel Ulysses T. Bragg, Director, US Army Special Projects.

Although they were thousands of miles away—Stein in the Amazon, Bragg in a stealth plane flying over the North Pole—both men appeared as if they were actually at the Kid Squad headquarters, a series of secret rooms under the basement of Pi's house.

"Kids, I have some terrible news," Colonel Bragg began, his booming voice echoing in the Kid Squad command chamber. "I'll let Dr. Stein elaborate. The fate of humankind rests on your shoulders."

Dr. Stein elaborated. The doctor told the Kid Squad about the comet and the calamity it would cause if it struck Earth.

"It is a catastrophe," he said. "In 132 hours, 6 minutes and 10 seconds, zee Earth and everything on it will, how do I say, go *poof* gone. The planet will be a lifeless rock circling zee sun, as cold as Neptune. Everything, including you and me, zee kitty over there, will be gone in zee instant."

Pi looked at Gadget. Gadget looked at Pi. Athena picked up D-Day and cradled him in her arms. Tank forgot about his game-winning hit.

"Holy guacamole!" Gadget finally said, breaking the uneasy silence.

"Indeed, young man," Colonel Bragg said. "Indeed."

Chapter 3
Think Bigger, Henry!

"Boss . . . Dr. Cobalt . . . can . . . can I . . . speak to you, sir, just for a . . . a second?"

Dr. Alowishus Cobalt swirled in his big leather chair, tearing his eyes from the satellite image of the speeding comet that he was sending on a collision course with Earth. The light from the gargantuan visorscreen (a cross between a 3-D TV and a computer) bounced off Cobalt's bald, fleshy head. It cast an eerie, dull light over his private office.

"What is it now, Henry?" Cobalt bellowed.

Henry hated talking to his boss and often found it hard to say what was on his mind. Dr. Cobalt was a mean, mean man. "Um . . . um . . . boss . . . I was talking to Maury. . . . You know Maury down in accounting? He's in charge of payroll."

"Spit it out, Henry," Cobalt said impatiently. "I don't have all day. I'm trying to scare the world and I have no time for distractions."

"Dr. Cobalt. Well . . . Maury told Loretta . . . you know . . . Loretta, sir . . . "

"HENRY. Get on with it!" Cobalt yelled.

"Well, boss, Maury told Loretta that . . . um . . . he intercepted a signal from Dr. Stein. Wasn't he your best friend at the university? Anyway, Dr. Stein was talking to that group of kids . . . you know the ones with that neat gadget. Well, it seems they're going to try to stop you and whatever, you, um, are planning . . . "

"Ah, yes," Cobalt said. "Ignatius and his Kid Squad. I bet that no-neck toy soldier Bragg is in on it, too. I rather expected this. I'm prepared, though, so you need not worry. Is there something else I can do for you, Henry? If not, you can go."

There *was* something else Cobalt could do for Henry. "Boss . . . Dr. Cobalt, sir . . . the guys and me were wonderin' about somethin'. Um, sir, I know you are very smart . . . but Pete in personnel says we're pulling a huge meteor toward Earth . . . "

"*Comet*, Henry," Cobalt corrected. "It's a comet, not a meteor. Meteors are small rocks or bits of dust that collide with Earth's atmosphere. Comets, Henry, are much, much larger. They're like dirty snowballs, huge globs of frozen water, rock, dust, and other things. Most comets exist in the far reaches of our solar system in an area called the Kuiper Belt. This one is traveling 100 miles every second and it's headed straight for Earth."

"Um, yes, sir, well, that comet . . . sir, if you don't mind me saying so, is getting awfully close. . . . That's what Pete told me. Pete says it's very big and something that big, well, sir, can mash us into tiny pebbles . . . can't it? How are we to, um, survive if that meteor . . . um, comet, hits Earth?

"I'm just askin', sir," Henry continued cautiously. "I know we're deep inside a mountain, but Pete says that a much smaller comet killed . . . um . . . the dinosaurs. Pete says it happened 65 million years ago. Dinosaurs were big, and we're, um, puny. I mean . . . do we have getaway cars or somethin'?"

"Ah, Henry. Think bigger, Henry!" Cobalt said. "You've been with me the longest, haven't you? Ten years now, correct?"

"Um, twelve sir. It's been twelve years. You hired me when we vaporized that bridge in London and kidnapped the prime minister."

"Ah, yes," Cobalt said smiling. "I remember. To your point: Yes, a comet that size will kill us all. It's moving at such a fantastic rate of speed that it will pulverize the planet. Remarkable, isn't it?

"But, you can tell Pete, Maury, Loretta, and anyone else, that they will be safe even if the world's leaders don't pay what I've asked. Everyone who works for me will escape. I promise."

"Even Eddie down in the cafeteria?" Henry wondered. "He makes a nice taco and spaghetti salad."

"Even Eddie," Cobalt said in exasperation.

"That's good, sir," Henry said. "Um, boss. You are the richest man I know. Why . . . why, um, sir, do you . . . want more money?"

Cobalt thought for a moment. It was an honest question from an honest man. Henry deserved an answer.

"Don't you see, Henry?" Cobalt said. "I couldn't care less about the money. I'm so filthy rich that I can't even spend all the money I've stolen over the years."

Cobalt let out a sinister giggle. "The point is, Henry, that they laughed at me. Those fools,

Ignatius, Bragg, all of them . . . they laughed at me. Ignatius didn't invent the Amulator . . . I did. That blackguard stole my idea . . . "

"The Amu . . . what, sir?" Henry asked.

"The Amulator. It can do wonderful, evil things . . . in the right hands, of course. It is the most powerful machine in the world. It can turn people invisible, stop an airplane in mid-flight, and even take you back through time to the day your grandmother was born. Would you like to see your grandmother as a little baby, Henry?"

"Oh, Dr. Cobalt that would be wonderful. She's eighty-four now, but, oh, I bet she was a pretty baby. I've seen pictures. She had long blonde curls, a pink . . . "

"Yes, Henry, that's all very nice," Cobalt interrupted. "The point is that the Amulator is the most important machine in the universe. It's hidden somewhere . . . I don't know where. But those little brats can activate it wherever and whenever they want from those access pads strapped to their wrists."

Cobalt stopped, took a deep breath, and

searched the file cabinet of his mind for a memory he would rather have forgotten. It was painful and made him even madder than usual.

"Ignatius and Bragg stopped me from using the Amulator. They sent me to prison, a simply detestable speck of an island for the criminally insane. Ha. Do I *look* insane to you, Henry?"

Not knowing what to say, Henry said nothing.

"Anyway, that peace-loving Ignatius decided to use the Amulator for good, not evil. Who does such things? Really! How boring. I was always smarter than Ignatius, and now the world will see. Everyone will know how smart I am."

Cobalt roared maniacally. It frightened Henry to the pit of his stomach, which, by the way, was filled with two helpings of Eddie's taco and spaghetti salad and a chunk of his wife's chocolate cake. Henry had never seen his boss act so . . . so . . . *Crazy* with a capital *C*.

"Um, sir . . . I have to, ah . . . go, sir . . . Maury's waiting to go on break," Henry stuttered.

"Not so fast, my old friend. I have an important mission for you."

Henry gulped. He hated "important missions." They were always dangerous. Henry wanted to retire in two years. Danger was certainly not his business.

"You see, in order to rule the universe, I need the Amulator, or at the very least, it has to be incapacitated. Do you know what *incapacitated* means, Henry?"

Henry did not, although he had a good idea.

"It means out of action," Cobalt said, answering his own question. "Can you help me? Can you find one of the Amulator access pads that those squirts from the Kid Squad wear around their wrists and bring it back to me?"

Henry thought for a moment. Cobalt's private office grew darker. His evil face glistened in the artificial light spilling out of the visorscreen.

"Better yet, bring me one of the kids. You know the one."

Henry thought for a moment. All he could picture was retiring, making birdhouses, and drinking his favorite drink—orange juice topped with whipped cream and sprinkles.

"Sure, boss," Henry said reluctantly.

"That's the spirit," Cobalt said with a sly smile.

With that, Henry slunk away in despair. If nothing else, he was a good soldier. He would do his duty. His birdhouses and orange drink would have to wait.

Chapter 4
Gadget Goes for a Walk

"Tell me again why we're up here?" Tank asked. He and Gadget were high above Webster's Corners in the bell tower of the Old South Church. As they looked out from their lofty perch, they could see the town green, Tank's house on Doolittle Street, Copernicus Middle School, the Shake & Stir, and the ball field where Tank had hit his game-winning home run the day before.

Webster's Corners was a nice place to live. It was small and quiet, nestled near a ring of hills that crawled up to a series of mountains. The town was leafy green in summer and snowy white in winter.

The people in Webster's Corners were nice, too. There was Gadget's Aunt Sally, who made the best raisin-walnut brownies in town. There was also Sophie Ann Mackenzie, whom Tank liked more than anyone else in the sixth grade. The only problem was that she was always talking to Kyle Witherbee—that dork burger with the fancy clothes and perfect hair.

"For the fourth time," Gadget began, "we're searching for Cobalt's tractor beam. If we find it, we can program the device to push the comet away from Earth, or so I think."

"Why don't we just use our Amulator to destroy the comet?" Tank chimed in.

Gadget shook his head. "The comet is out of the Amulator's range," Gadget said. "By the time that dirty snowball gets in range it will be too late to use the Amulator. In the meantime, we, along with Pi and Athena, are trying to locate the tractor beam."

"Where are they, anyway?" Tank asked.

"Athena's in orbit on one side of the world.

Pi is in orbit on the other side. They're using the Amulator's transportsphere so they can float above the planet safely."

"So, how does this all work?" Tank asked as if he cared about the details.

Gadget gave out an annoyed sigh. "By coordinating our vectors and calculating the axis point, we can find the location of the tractor beam," he said. "The beam throws off a lot of energy. By using the Amulator's access pads, we can triangulate and pinpoint the source of power. That will tell us where Cobalt's hideout is."

Tank scratched his noggin, messing up his carefully combed blond hair. "Coordinating our what? Triangulating who? What in the wide world of sports is a vector?"

Tank was smart. He knew what was going on. He just liked to tease Gadget.

Gadget usually loved explaining how things worked. In fact, he lived for it. He was always the first to raise his hand in Mrs. Bower's science class, and the first to figure out a math problem. He could make a mini-laser from a light bulb, a car battery, and a telescope. He could build a radio from a coffee can and some wires.

Now was not the time to school Tank on the ins and outs of tractor beams, Amulators, and diabolical comets that have run amok. Tank was his friend, though. Gadget took out his pen and pencil and pushed his glasses up on his nose.

"Look here," he started. "This circle I'm drawing is Earth. This X is Athena. She's hovering over Africa in her transportsphere. This X is Pi. She's soaring above the North Pole. This X is you and me, here in Webster's Corners. When we adjust our access pads, the Amulator will send out a signal from each location searching for the tractor beam. The three signals will intersect at the spot where the tractor beam is located, just like this," Gadget said finishing his drawing.

"Where is that Amulator anyway?" Tank asked, snickering because he knew its location was a secret, even to Pi, who ran the Kid Squad. He loved teasing Gadget.

"Really, Tank?" Gadget asked, not waiting for an answer. "You know Dr. Stein and Colonel Bragg are the only ones who know where it is. That's why they gave us these new access pads. We can use the Amulator anytime, anywhere."

Gadget looked at his watch. "Everyone should be in position right about now. Okay, ready. Keep your fingers crossed."

Gadget pressed a button on his access pad. Athena, high over Africa, pressed a button on her access pad. Pi, floating over the top of the world, did the same. The Amulator, wherever it was, powered up. It calculated an amazing amount of data every second.

Gadget waited.

Athena waited.

Pi waited.

Tank waited, chewing his fingernails.

One minute turned into two. Two minutes turned into five. Five turned into ten.

Nothing.

"Holy guacamole!" Gadget said. "It's not working. The Amulator is not picking up the tractor beam's location. Cobalt has found a way to hide the tractor beam even from the Amulator."

"What does that mean?" Tank asked.

"It means the tractor beam could be anywhere. For all I know it could be under this very church."

"Nah, I don't think so," Tank said. "Last week Teddy McAllister and I snuck into the basement. All that's down there are old church benches and some cobwebs."

"Tank, don't be a dork burger!" Gadget yelled. "It also means we're doomed if we don't figure out something else."

"Doomed, as in *kaput*," Tank tried to joke, mimicking Dr. Stein's thick German accent.

Gadget wasn't laughing.

"Don't worry, Gad," Tank said. "We'll solve this problem. We always do."

Gadget wasn't so sure this time. He was confused and angry for not being able to find a simple solution. He was always good at figuring things out. This time though . . .

"Meet me back at headquarters," Gadget ordered Tank. "Pi and Athena will be there in a few minutes. We'll have to find another way."

"Where are you going?"

"I'm going to take a walk and think."

The friends climbed down the stairs of the Old South Church. Tank followed the sidewalk one way, Gadget another. He had a lot to think about.

¤

Main Street in Webster's Corners was like any other Main Street in any other town. Although Gadget was walking down the neat little avenue, his mind was somewhere else.

He didn't notice the shady oaks and maples that kept the sidewalk cool from the June sun. He didn't smell the fresh razzleberry pie Mrs. Hornsnout had just placed on the windowsill to cool. He didn't feel the warm breeze blowing from the west or hear the sweet whistle of a cardinal pecking away at Mrs. Goldbert's bird feeder. And he certainly didn't see the odd-looking fellow walking toward him.

The man was wearing black pants, a black shirt, and black shoes. He even wore a black ski cap rolled up on the top of his head. He was round and desperately needed a shave. He kept licking his lips as if he were nervous.

Finally, the man stopped Gadget in the middle of the sidewalk.

"Son," the strange man said. "Son, can you tell me where Sycamore Street is?"

The man's voice shook Gadget's mind awake. For a split second, the boy forgot about the tractor beam and the comet. "Sycamore Street?" he asked.

"Yes, I . . . um . . . I'm looking for Sycamore Street," the man said. "592 Sycamore to be exact."

"That's on the other side of town," Gadget answered. "It's a half-hour walk from here."

"Um . . . I didn't know, um, that," the man said. Gadget could see the man was sweating. Why was he wearing a ski cap in early June? It had to be eighty degrees outside. He didn't seem like the brightest bulb on the Christmas tree, Gadget thought, but he tried not to judge others.

"I'm sort of, you know, new. That's it, I'm new around here," the man said, stumbling nervously over his words. "Perhaps you can show me, um, you know . . . show me the way."

"I don't think so," Gadget said nervously. "I don't talk to strangers and I especially don't go anywhere with them. Now if you'll excuse me, I have some important work to do."

"Oh, I'm not a stranger," the man said as Gadget tried to walk away. "We, um, you know, have a mutual friend . . . Dr. Alowishus Cobalt."

The name gobsmacked Gadget. It echoed in his brain like a bad dream. Gadget knew he was in trouble.

"Holy guacamole," he said.

Gadget turned to run. Before his legs could move, however, the strange man pulled a pen-like canister from his back pocket and shoved it in Gadget's face. The man pulled the ski cap down over his eyes and mouth and squeezed the canister.

Gadget tried hard not to breathe. He put one hand, then two, over his mouth. It was useless. Gadget breathed in. It was knockout gas.

Gadget coughed. He choked. He hacked. His knees buckled. His legs wobbled. His hands shook. His eyes fluttered. Just before Gadget slumped to the ground, he heard the man mutter: "I'm so sorry, son. I'm so, so sorry. I didn't want to do this, but um, orders are orders as my friend Maury says. Oh, gosh. Oh, gosh. I just want to retire and build birdhouses."

Chapter 5
The **Evil Genius** Speaks

The Kid Squad command center was abuzz with activity. Pi and Athena were using satellites to locate the tractor beam by trying to determine any rise or fall in Earth's magnetic field.

Dr. Stein, or more correctly, a holophone image of him, paced the floor frantically, using his genius to figure out various mathematical formulas relating to the impending collision of the comet.

Tank was monitoring the communication channels, trying to hone in on one of Cobalt's transmissions to his henchmen.

As for D-Day, well he was doing what he loved to do—lounging near a warm computer screen, a bowl of milk at the ready.

"Dr. Stein," Pi said. "I have an idea. We're running out of time trying to locate this tractor beam. What if we use the Amulator to *stop time*? We did it before when General Orpheus attacked the White House. Why don't we do the same thing now?"

"*Nein, nein, nein,*" Dr. Stein shouted. "No, no, no. It can't be done! Stopping time with zee Amulator will destroy zee world faster than zee comet. Haven't I taught you kids, how do you say, zee basics?"

Pi looked at Dr. Stein as if he were talking gibberish. Her dark eyes widened as she spoke: "How could stopping time destroy the world?"

"Let me explain," Dr. Stein began. "Zee Amulator can stop zee time, but only, how you say, in zee limited area. Yes, zee limited area. It only stops time for zee people nearest you . . . "

"Can't we adjust it to stop time for everyone, except us?" Athena said. "That would give us time to find the tractor beam and direct the comet away from Earth."

"*Nein, nein, nein* again," Dr. Stein said. "No, no, no. If we stop zee time all around zee world, what do you think will happen?"

No one answered.

"Eh, no one knows, *unglaublich,* unbelievable. Use your heads. How many hours are in zee day?" Dr. Stein asked.

"I know that," Tank answered, raising his hand as if he were in class. "There are twenty-four hours in a day."

"*Wunderbar*, wonderful," Dr. Stein said. "Someone was paying attention in school. Why is that?"

"It takes twenty-four hours for Earth to make one complete revolution, or turn, on its axis," Tank added.

"*Wunderbar*, young man," Dr. Stein cheered.

"What do you think will happen if we stop time for zee entire planet?"

Again, no one knew the answer.

"We would stop zee world from spinning," Dr. Stein explained. "Zee only way to stop time for everyone is to stop zee world from revolving on zee axis. What would happen if zee world stopped spinning?"

No one dared interrupt.

"Everything not fixed to zee Earth would continue to rotate around at zee same rate of speed," he offered. "Buildings would collapse, zee oceans would swamp zee land in large tidal waves. As for you, me, and zee kitty over there, we would be tossed around like, how you say, rag dolls. So, my young friends, what would happen if zee Earth stopped zee spinning?"

"*Kaput!*" Pi said.

"*Kaput!*" Tank offered.

"*Kaput!*" Athena whispered.

"*Kaput!*" Dr. Stein yelled, his unkempt hair flailing about. "That is why we have to continue zee search to find zee tractor beam. Pi, you're zee leader of zee Kid Squad. You must use zee Amulator and travel closer to zee comet. It is dangerous, but perhaps you can locate zee tractor beam from outer space."

"I don't know, Dr. Stein," Pi said defeated. "I think we're licked. I wish Gad were here. Where is he, anyway? He should have been here hours ago."

Suddenly, all the TV monitors and computer screens in the command center went blank. It only lasted for a few seconds. Then Cobalt appeared. His double-chinned face wasn't just on one or two screens, but all of them. In fact, the mad doctor was on every TV, computer, cell phone, and tablet screen in the world. He was even on the radio.

He appeared larger than life on a huge screen in Times Square. Those living in Moscow and Rome saw his bald head and menacing face too.

He was on every scoreboard in every stadium around the world. He spoke in English. He spoke Italian, Mandarin, and Spanish. He chatted in French and rambled in Swahili. No one could escape his message, unless of course, they were asleep, which by the way, half the world was. They'd have to get the news later on. Pi and Athena looked at the TV. Tank stared at his computer.

"Good evening, my fellow human beings. Forgive the intrusion. This shall only take a minute or two. My name is Dr. Alowishus Cobalt and I'd like to let you in on a little secret. Don't you just love secrets? My sister used to tell me secrets all the time, but only when I pulled her hair. Hi, sis! By the way, I won't be home for the holidays.

"Anywho . . . within the next few minutes or so, Earth's astronomers will see something in their telescopes they have never seen before.

They will see a comet where no comet was yesterday. At first, the comet's position will confuse them. They'll search their data banks to see if it has appeared before. They will do the math and double check it. They will run the numbers again, and again, and again. The answer will remain the same no matter how many times they add, subtract, divide, or multiply.

"And what is that answer? I'll save everyone a lot of time. The comet is hurling toward Earth at a fantastic rate of speed. It's so fast, well, I can't even imagine it myself. And it's so big, too. When I hooked on to it, I couldn't believe what a whopper I had landed. I was so happy that I named it the Comet of Doom. Has a nice ring to it, don't you think? I'm getting ahead of myself, though."

Cobalt took a deep breath and a big swig of water before continuing his diabolical rant.

"Here's the scoop. Simply, the Comet of Doom will strike Earth about four days from now, give or take an hour or two. I'm going to see if I can speed it up. Oh, wait. I'm getting ahead of myself again.

"Here's how I did it. Are you ready? This is so cool. I hooked on to the comet with this awesome tractor beam I made. I know . . . I know . . . 'tractor beam' is so, well, *Star Trek*. Penny and Gert down in advertising couldn't figure out a better name either, so we went with it.

"The bottom line is that I'm pulling the comet toward Earth like a fisherman reels in a trophy-sized bass. Unfortunately, when I pull this sucker into the boat, you will, well, I can't put this delicately . . . perish.

"Oh yes, the Comet of Doom is moving fast enough and is large enough that Earth is going to go the way of the dinosaurs, which by the way, aren't around anymore because of, you guessed it—a collision with a comet or a super-big asteroid.

"Destroying stuff is a little hobby of mine. This is my biggest project yet, and it seems to be working wonderfully. Isn't that awesome? I mean, who'd have *thunk* it?

"I'm sorry, it's awesome for me, but not for you, I suppose. I decided to warn you a couple of days ago by telling a certain scientist. I really, really did. Scout's honor. Pinkie swear. Dr. Ignatius Newton Stein has known about the comet for two days but has not told you about it yet. I guess he and his pal Colonel Bragg wanted to keep it a surprise. SURPRISE!

"In all honesty, they probably didn't want to cause a panic. *Panic shmanick,* that's what I say. I'm telling you all this now because you can stop it. Oh, yes. It's quite simple. Want to hear how? I'll tell you right after a word from our sponsor. I'm joking. This is a commercial-free show."

Cobalt was having a wonderfully sinister time telling the world of his plan. He smirked, smiled, and laughed. It was a big game to him.

"Frankly, I didn't think my plan would ever get to this point. Yet, here we are. All you have to do is pay me what I ask and I'll turn the comet harmlessly around. I might even steer it toward the sun. Who knows! I can bat it around like a ping-pong ball, or at least I think I can. It's all new territory for me.

"What I do know is that in four days or less, depending on how I feel and whether I get a cup of coffee in the morning, Earth will be a smoking cinder. The planet may or may not smoke. It's only a theory . . . but an educated one. It might seem as if I'm off my rocker, but I am totally sane and deadly serious."

Cobalt's voice became grave. His beady eyes squinted smaller if that was possible.

"Pay me $200 billion in gold and the comet goes away. Oh yes, I almost forgot. Ignatius and Bragg have to cough up that little device of theirs. They know the one I want. It's not much to ask for, considering what's at stake. If your leaders do not pay me, I think you know what will happen. And it *will* happen. I can assure you.

"I know, I know. You're thinking I'm just some crazy reality TV show star, the Mad Scientist of Venus or some such. I'm not. I cannot stress that point enough. Take what I say seriously. I'm a genius, smarter than Ignatius, Bragg, all of them. I'm not bad looking either. I like long walks on the beach . . . I love puppies, and I'm an Aries . . . send your photos in an e-mail to . . . sorry, I get carried away sometimes. Ha!

"Google me if you don't believe what I am telling you. Go ahead! I'm all over the Web.

Newspapers, magazines, blogs. *TIME* did a nice spread a couple of years ago when I tried to swamp Europe with my Tsunami Maker. The photos were very flattering.

"Some would say I'm famous. Others would say infamous. You decide. It's all the same to me. Look up *evil* in the dictionary and you'll see my picture.

"You get the idea. Ignatius knows how to get in touch with me. I have to go now. I have so much to do and so little time to do it."

Cobalt laughed bizarrely.

"I want you all to have a nice day, if you can. So long, *auf Wiedersehen*, *arrivederci*, *adios*, toodles, see you later alligator."

The transmission cut itself off and everyone's electronic devices returned to normal. Yet, there was something odd in the Kid Squad command center. As Cobalt had talked, D-Day had stood on his hind paws staring at the

TV. He made weird rasping sounds, as if he had a mouse stuck in his throat. The sounds grew louder and louder with each of Cobalt's passing words.

"What's that cat's problem?" Tank finally asked.

"I'm not sure," Athena said. "He acts this way sometimes. You know he's psychic or something. He goes into these trances. He knows something that we don't know. I wish he could talk."

D-Day couldn't talk, but he could run. He jumped down and ran out the door as if he were being chased by a dog. Athena ran after him. D-Day did know something no one else did. Athena had to find out what it was.

Chapter 6
Cobalt's Madness

"How was I?" Cobalt asked the prisoner. "Did they shoot my best side? I hope so. I always wanted to be a TV star and an Internet sensation. Now I am. I might have stumbled on a new career."

Cobalt smiled, then turned from his prisoner and looked out over his domain. Bats lived in caves and so did Alowishus Cobalt. While bat caves were dark and musty, Cobalt's cave was a place of dry, gray rock and bright light, heated and cooled by geothermal energy. That's energy from inside Earth. Located in an abandoned mine, the cave was as large as five football fields.

A series of hallways snaked through the cavern like a corn maze without the corn.

There were many rooms, elevators, escalators, and a cafeteria that served taco and spaghetti salad every Tuesday and Thursday. The tuna melt with cheddar cheese and chips wasn't bad either.

Cobalt and his team of extremely dangerous people busied themselves inside the cavern 24-7, as one would expect when threatening to destroy Earth.

Cobalt loved the cave. It was the shining jewel in a series of secret lairs. It was the place where he conducted his sinful business. The main control room was a marvel of science, with machines, computers, and other inventions that no one knew existed, or could exist. Yes, Alowishus Cobalt was mad, but he was also fiendishly smart.

Every day, Cobalt smiled to himself as he looked out the large windows of his office, which was carved into the side of the cave above the main control room. The windows were bulletproof. They were bombproof. Not even a missile from a handheld launcher could make a dent.

Cobalt's minions were happy to do their boss's bidding. Cobalt paid them handsomely. They repaid him with loyalty. Some were ultra-super-sophisticated robots with electronic brains and arms that snapped on. Cobalt didn't have to pay them, he only had to recharge their batteries.

Little did the prisoner know that Cobalt's office had an invisible entrance to the tractor beam room. The beam was powered by a nuclear reactor infinitely more powerful than any other nuclear reactor in the world.

The Comet of Doom was by far Cobalt's greatest caper, and he didn't want anything to go wrong. It dwarfed all the other crimes that had made Cobalt a most excellent mad scientist.

He had spent years planning the dastardly deed, and he wanted to share it with someone who would appreciate all his hard work—Arthur Thomas "Gadget" Williams.

"Arthur, my dear friend," Cobalt said. "Do you know why I brought you here?"

Henry had chained Gadget to a special chair in Cobalt's office. Heavy-duty steel bracelets attached to the arms of the chair locked Gadget's wrists. The knockout gas had worn off about a half hour earlier. The boy had broken his glasses when he fell to the ground. Henry, who stood guard, was trying to tape them together as best he could.

Still, Gadget didn't know where he was. He just knew he was in trouble.

"Holy guacamole!" Gadget shouted. "I suspect you kidnapped me to steal the access pad for the Amulator. With the Amulator out of the way, you can do as you wish."

"My, my," Cobalt said. "You do think me one-dimensional, do you not?"

"I do," answered Gadget, "and evil."

"I do want the Amulator. But that is secondary to what I really want. Do you know what I really want, Arthur?"

"To destroy the world," Gadget answered.

"You do think me a fiend, don't you? Arthur, Arthur, Arthur. I have great plans. Great life-changing plans. I want you to help me build the greatest empire the universe has ever seen. Do you think I'm a genius, Arthur?"

"I think you're mad."

"Mad . . . genius . . . it's all the same. Look, Arthur. Look at all the things no mortal being can do—except me."

Cobalt waved his hand, turned his head, and looked out the office windows, admiring his handiwork.

"Arthur, my dear young man, only a few people in the world appreciate such genius, and you're one of them, no matter how much you despise me. Out of all the Kid Squad members, you are the only one who knows greatness. Who else but I would even dare lasso a comet and send it hurling toward Earth?"

Gadget looked perplexed. He didn't realize that Cobalt had been spying on him or the other members of the Kid Squad.

"Arthur, you and I are very much alike. We have vision. We create. We see the impossible and make it possible. Not even Ignatius Stein, with all his fancy awards and prizes, can do such things."

"I'm not like you!" Gadget yelled, his voice cracking. "You're a mean, insane, violent man who thinks he can play with the world as if it were a pawn in a chess set. No, Dr. Cobalt, we are not alike."

"Be that as it may," Cobalt said unfazed, "do me a kindness as you sit here as my guest, and please hear me out. I beg you."

Cobalt paused. His face grew serious. The lines in his pale forehead wrinkled like a dried prune. His pea-sized eyes welled with tears.

"I can do many things, but I cannot make myself live forever. Oh, I'm trying, but it is hard work. I will surely fail. This old ticker of mine isn't as strong as it used to be." Cobalt thumped his chest.

"But you, my dear boy, are young. You have your whole life ahead of you. This can all be yours."

Once again, Cobalt waved his hand to show Gadget the wonders of the cave below.

"Join me and I will teach you all that I know. You and I can rule the world, Arthur."

"Holy guacamole! I'm not stupid. You don't want to rule the world, you want to destroy it."

"Ah, yes, there is that," Cobalt admitted. "Let me rephrase. Arthur, Earth is nothing more than a speck of dust. Join me and rule the universe. The universe is vast. With the Amulator in our possession, it can be ours. I've seen many worlds in my travels. They can all be dominated . . . dominated by the two of us."

Cobalt stopped, turned from Gadget, and looked wistfully out the windows. Below him, the control room was buzzing as workers and robots prepared for the final countdown.

"I, Alowishus Cobalt, son of Becky and Peter Cobalt, will be Master of the Universe someday. That's such a nice title, Master of the Universe. I already had it printed on my business cards. And to think those stupid little fools in high school didn't elect me most likely to succeed."

Gadget had had enough of these maniacal ramblings. He struggled to free himself but gave up after a minute or two. The steel bracelets were too tight. They cut deep into Gadget's wrists.

"If I join you and help you steal the Amulator, will you send the comet away from Earth?" Gadget asked the evil scientist.

Cobalt put a finger to his chin and thought. He nodded and said, "Interesting proposition, young man. I wasn't prepared for that. Interesting, indeed. Let me think for a moment."

The room grew silent. Henry, who was standing out of sight, nervously shuffled his feet. He hoped that Cobalt would agree to Gadget's offer. Henry could then retire and make birdhouses.

"No," Cobalt finally said. "I will not stop the comet from striking Earth, not even if you agree to join me. Henry, switch on visorscreen Number 2."

The huge visorscreen clicked to life high above Cobalt's desk. Cobalt spun Gadget's chair so it faced the screen. Gadget looked up and saw his friend Pi traveling through space trying to catch up to the speeding comet. She was doing what Dr. Stein had ordered her to do.

"This is your friend Pi, isn't it?" Cobalt said. "She's using the Amulator to travel through space so she can try to find the source of the tractor beam. Ingenious, really.

"Frankly, she'll probably be successful. No matter how hard I tried, I could not find a way to cloak the tractor beam once it passed through the asteroid belt. All those asteroids between Mars and Jupiter are causing it to shimmy and shake. The Amulator will pick up those distortions once Pi is in range.

"However, I am the brightest crayon in the box, and as such, anticipated this."

Cobalt sighed.

"Let me put my cards on the table, Arthur. I will not stop the comet from striking Earth even if you join me. What kind of evil genius would I be? Not a very good one, that's for sure. Everyone would laugh, especially all my friends at the Evil Genius Club.

"What I will do instead, is save all of your friends. If you join me, I will make sure that all the Kid Squad members survive the collision. We will all go to Mars and live happily ever after. My hideout on the Red Planet isn't as big as this one, but it has an Olympic-sized pool, an all-night buffet, and even a mini-golf course.

"You and I will conquer the universe from there, Arthur. We really don't need the Amulator, I suppose. I can try to build another one, but Stein was able to make it work so much better than I could have ever imagined. It's up to you. Join me and live . . . or stay here and watch your friends disappear . . . one Kid Squad member at time . . . beginning with Pi, the leader of your annoying little group."

Cobalt then let out one of his horrible laughs. It made Henry tremble. Henry had heard Cobalt laugh a million times before, but this laugh was different. Henry started to think that things weren't going to end well. He would never retire and make birdhouses. He would never see his wife again. *Gosh, what am I going to do?* Henry thought. *What* can *I do?*

Chapter 7
Pi in the Sky

Pi zipped through the solar system in the transportsphere. She couldn't help but stare in wonder at the glorious outstretched arms of the Milky Way. The galaxy looked as if someone had taken a brush, dipped it in magical paint, and spread it across a dark canvas.

Pi spotted Polaris, the North Star. It was at the end of the Little Dipper's handle. She also saw Alpha Centauri, the closest star system to Earth's sun.

Although fascinated by these wonderful objects, Pi's main concern was the flaming ball of light she was chasing. The comet Cobalt had unleashed against Earth was beautiful, but deadly.

The sun's solar winds pushed the gas and dust away from the comet, causing it to form a long, fiery tail known as a coma. The coma glowed bright in the blackness of space. In less than a day, people on Earth would be able to see the terrifying traveler streak across the night sky. A day later, the flaming ball of ice would appear even larger. After that . . . well, Pi didn't want to think about what could happen.

Pi's job now was to get as close to the comet as possible. At the right moment, she'd program the Amulator to locate the tractor beam. She would then radio Tank at the Kid Squad headquarters. Tank would alert Dr. Stein and Colonel Bragg. If all went according to plan, Bragg's elite unit of soldiers would quickly descend on Cobalt's base and send the comet on a new course far away from Earth. But Pi had been a Kid Squad member long enough to know that things never went according to plan.

As Pi floated weightless and alone among the stars, the transportsphere began to tumble wildly out of control. Pi was not prepared. She foolishly had her seat belt off. The transportsphere was a big, complicated, machine-like bubble. Although you could see through it, the ship contained many interesting devices.

The transportsphere was propelled by the Amulator. It could take any member of the Kid Squad on a journey through the cosmos faster than a modern rocket. The kids could pack the transportsphere with dried food to eat, water to drink, and oxygen to breathe. The ship could land on a planet, travel through a wall of fire, or swim underwater faster than any submarine.

Despite all that, the attack on the transportsphere continued. It spun, jerked, and tumbled, shaking Pi as a puppy shakes a pull toy. Pi tried to steady the craft, but she couldn't reach the adjuster buttons. The spinning was making her sick.

Back on Earth, Tank watched on a video screen from the Kid Squad command center as the transportsphere shuddered violently. Abruptly, the screen went blank.

"Command center to transportsphere!" Tank shouted frantically into his microphone. "Command center to transportsphere! Pi come in! Pi come in!"

Pi could not come in. The leader of the Kid Squad was losing the battle. She finally reached the adjusters, but they did not work. She tried everything she knew. Some invisible force was causing the craft to act violently. Pi knew who was responsible—Cobalt. He was trying to stop her from finding the source of the tractor beam.

"Command center to transportsphere!" Tank roared once again. "Command center to transportsphere. Pi come in! Pi come in! Are you there? Are you okay?"

Pi could hear but could not respond. The transportsphere spun so rapidly that the force of its rotation had her pinned against the side of the craft, like water in a spinning bucket.

She knew if the ship stopped quickly, the force would knock her back to the center of the transportsphere. And that's exactly what happened. The ship came to a halt. Pi flew toward the center of the sphere and smacked her head against the command chair.

Dazed, a bit confused, and with a bloody red gash starting to open over her eye, Pi managed to crawl to her seat and strap herself in good and tight.

Once again, the transportsphere spun. Pi tried to take control. The ship would not respond. It was as if a great hand were playing with the round vessel, tossing it up, down, and around as a child tosses a ball.

All of a sudden, from the corner of her eye, Pi spotted asteroids. The transportsphere was being tossed right at them! Pi had entered the asteroid belt, the rock-strewn region of the solar system between Mars and Jupiter. Some rocks were as big as small moons. Others were the size of basketballs.

Pi activated the transportsphere's deflection shields. The smaller asteroids harmlessly bounced off the craft. But Pi knew she was in a jam.

"Command center to transportsphere!" Tank screamed. "Command center to transportsphere. Pi come in! Pi come in! Are you there? Are you okay? Pi!"

Silence. Pi still could not answer. She used every bit of Kid Squad training she had to keep from being bowled over by an asteroid. Cobalt, however, still had his sinister grip on the ship. There was nothing Pi could do. *How was Cobalt able to override the Amulator to toss the transportsphere back and forth?* she thought.

The answer finally came. *Cobalt had his dirty mitts on an access pad—Gadget's access pad. That's where Gadget had disappeared to! Gadget is Cobalt's prisoner. Cobalt is using the Amulator against me.*

There was only one way to get out of this mess. Someone needed to turn the Amulator off. It would render all the access pads unusable, even the one Cobalt had stolen.

I can't turn the Amulator off from here, Pi thought. *It has to be done from the command center.* Dr. Stein couldn't pull the plug, nor could Bragg. Both men were at the United Nations in New York City, briefing leaders on the comet.

Pi needed to talk to Tank. But she could no longer hear his shouts. The radio was out. Cobalt had shut off communication to the whirling transportsphere.

Think, Tank. Think . . . switch off the Amulator.

Pi hoped that Tank would figure it out. He was a smart ballplayer, the best in school. He also dazzled in biology class. He knew the human body inside and out. His father was a world-famous heart surgeon. All that knowledge came in handy when Tank and Pi had to miniaturize themselves to operate on the heart of the King of Sherpa, a pint-sized monarch who ruled the hidden nation of Bungo Bongo.

Think, Tank. Think. Pull the switch! Now! Pull the switch!

C'mon, Tank. Use your head. Turn the Amulator off.

Pi pushed her hair from the side of her face. In front of her was an asteroid as big as the Empire State Building. It was moving fast. If it hit . . . *kaput*! Even the transportsphere's protective shields had a limit. Pi was doomed, she thought. She took a deep breath and waited for the collision.

It never came. Instead, the bubble-like craft shot straight up (although there is no up in space, or down for that matter) and out of the asteroid belt. It spun, rolled, and came to a slow stop.

"Tank," Pi muttered to herself. "He must have figured it out. Good ole Tank."

That's exactly what had happened. Tank pulled the override switch at headquarters, which switched off the Amulator. That allowed the transportsphere to rocket out of the asteroid belt. He hoped it wasn't too late.

"Command center to transportsphere," Tank said. "Command center to transportsphere! Pi come in! Pi come in! Can you hear me?"

"I can," Pi said, breathing a sigh of relief. "Thanks, Tank. I was about to become cosmic roadkill. You saved my life."

"Nothing to it, Pi. I'm glad you're safe."

"Me, too," Pi said. "Cobalt's got Gadget and the access pad."

"I figured," Tank said. "As long as Cobalt can use the Amulator, we will have to keep the device off from here. That means *we* can't use the Amulator. If we can't use the Amulator, then we can't stop him or that darn comet."

"I know," a discouraged Pi responded. "We still don't know where his hideout is. And I didn't have a chance to get a fix on the tractor beam. It doesn't look good."

"Nonsense," Tank said with a hefty dose of optimism. "Gadget's obviously with Cobalt. Gad will figure out a way to stop him. He'll get us word. I know he will. He'll probably strap a message to a carrier pigeon and build a tiny jet pack out of a soda can so the bird can fly faster. We'll win the ball game. We always do. We're undefeated. Come back home and we'll decide what to do next."

"Sounds good," Pi said. "See you soon."

Pi settled into the transportsphere's chair and sped back to Earth. She watched the big blue marble of her home planet get closer with each passing minute. Big, white, puffy clouds blanketed parts of South America. A storm was forming just off the western coast of Africa. The Pacific Ocean was a bright blue-green.

Sure is beautiful, Pi thought. *Cobalt's comet will make that big blue marble as black as coal. As black as coal.*

Chapter 8
D-Day Leads the Way

Although he was a little cat, D-Day's tiny legs sure could walk a long way. Athena had followed her feline friend across Webster's Corners. They crossed streams and bridges, scampered down dusty roads, and trotted through the forest.

It was a painful trip. Athena cut her arms and legs trying to walk across a field of bramble. She fell and scraped her knee after slipping on a rock. She grew angrier with every step.

"D-Day, you're leading me on a wild goose chase!" Athena cried at one point.

All D-Day could do was give out a short "merrrowww" and keep on moving.

"Pi is going to be so mad that we've been

walking around all day doing nothing," Athena whined. "D-Day, where are we going?"

D-Day followed his cat sense, which allowed him to see things others could not. Some people believe that cats have nine lives. D-Day had a sixth sense.

He couldn't talk, so Athena was left to wonder what was going through his mind. She was always cheery and sweet, but not today.

Athena's archaeologist parents named their only daughter after the Greek goddess of courage, wisdom, and inspiration. At this moment, Athena felt none of these things. She was hot, dirty, and thirsty. She grew tired of picking tiny bits of briar out of her long hair.

The pair walked for what seemed like an eternity, D-Day's little white legs moving faster the closer he came to the final destination—wherever that might be.

"We're lost, aren't we, you little fur ball?" Athena said with a huge sigh. "I have no idea where we are. The Amulator is out of power for some reason, so I can't even tap into its satellite positioning app. How are we going to get back? D-Day, you're a bad, bad kitty."

The cat stopped as suddenly as he had begun this painful journey. If he were a hunting dog, D-Day would have raised a front paw and pointed. Yet D-Day wasn't a dog. *Thank goodness*, he thought. He was a cat. So, he did what cats do when they see or sense something out of the ordinary. He stared straight ahead and cried a loud, piercing "meowww."

"Meowww," he cried again.

"What is it now?" Athena yelled. "You dragged me to the ends of the earth. My feet hurt. My shirt is covered with little black things, and I just picked a tick off my shoulder."

Athena walked to where D-Day had stopped and looked over a row of shrubs. "Wow, we're near the old silver mine at the bottom of Klondike Mountain. My dad took me here once to look for artifacts. What are we doing here?"

It didn't take long for Athena to answer her own question. The entrance to the abandoned mine had long been boarded up. Now it was wide open. A *No Trespassing* sign lay on the ground. If that wasn't enough to convince Athena that something odd was going on, she saw five armed guards standing near the old mine's entrance.

"What are those guards doing here?" Athena whispered.

Athena's eyes looked like two saucers when she focused. "You know who those guards are, D-Day? They're Cobalt's robo sentries. They're armed with Freeze Ray guns. I think . . . I think this is Cobalt's hideout. Good job, D-Day. When we get back, I'm going to give you a can of sardines!"

D-Day purred excitedly. He loved sardines.

"Okay . . . okay . . . let me think, let me think, let me think," Athena said eagerly. "If Cobalt's

robo sentries are guarding the entrance to the old silver mine, then Cobalt has to be inside. If Cobalt is inside, then the tractor beam is inside, too. If the tractor beam is inside, we can figure out how to turn it off. If we turn it off, we can save the planet. Sweet! Who's better than us, cat?"

Then a thought crossed Athena's mind. Her freckled face grew solemn. "Gadget is in there, isn't he, D-Day?" Athena asked. "OMG. You sensed Gadget when you were watching Cobalt on TV! Oh, D-Day, you're one smart kitty, my BFF if ever I had one."

Athena wished she had an army of BFFs right now, but she didn't. What was she going to do? The access pad to the Amulator wasn't working, so she couldn't teleport herself or blast her way into the mine. She couldn't even use the device to turn herself invisible. Athena loved being invisible.

The situation was even more desperate because Athena had left her cell phone at headquarters. She couldn't text Pi or Tank to tell them the location of Cobalt's secret hideout. She couldn't get on Spacebook and alert Colonel Bragg and Dr. Stein, either.

"I'm such a dork burger with cheese," Athena said to herself. "I always have my cell phone. That means it's up to us, D-Day. Gadget is in there and he needs our help. If we can find another way inside, then we can free Gadget and turn that tractor beam into an epic fail."

"Merowww," D-Day answered, rubbing up against Athena's leg.

"Let's get going, my little fur ball," she said. "You lead the way."

¤

Gadget was in a pickle. He was in a jam. He was in a fix. He was up a stream without a paddle. No matter how he sliced it, Gadget was in one big mess.

The brainiest brainiac at Copernicus Middle School was alone, a prisoner in an evil genius lair. He figured it was nearly three o'clock in the afternoon. School had just let out. If all was right in the world, he and his friends would trot downtown to the library, finish their homework, and if there was time, explore the vast shelves of books that smelled, oh, so wonderful.

The world wasn't right—not today. Gadget guessed his friends and their parents were more than scared, wondering if they could escape the comet that was four days away. It was useless. There was no place to hide.

Gadget was alone and frightened. No one knew where he was. In fact, he didn't know where he was. He was a prisoner trapped in a room and strapped to a chair. As far as he could tell, there was only one way out of the room, a sliding steel door. But there was no place to go even if he could escape. For all Gadget knew, he was in the middle of Antarctica.

Just then, the sliding door opened with a loud *whoosh*! Henry walked in carrying a tray of food.

"I thought you might like to eat something," Henry said matter-of-factly. "I'm sure you haven't had anything to eat all day."

"I'm not hungry," Gadget lied. "You can take it away."

"There are some tasty treats here," Henry said smiling. "Eddie made them special. There's a peanut butter and yogurt sandwich, a glass of chocolate milk, a fruit cup, and Eddie's very own taco and spaghetti salad."

Gadget did not say a word. Henry stood alone in the silence of the room. He put the tray on the floor. His smile vanished.

"I want to tell you something," Henry said. "I'm, um, you know, sorry for kidnapping you and spraying your, um, face with that nasty knockout gas."

"Why did you do that?" Gadget asked.

"Orders are orders as my best friend Maury says. Do you know Maury? He's a sweet guy. He has three kids and four grandchildren."

"You know what Cobalt is up to, right Henry?" Gadget asked.

Henry didn't like thinking about what his boss was up to, but think about it was all Henry did. His always jolly face became grim. His eyes were moist.

"The boss says once he gets his money and that Amu-thingamabob, he'll stop that nasty meteor, um, comet, right in its tracks. Everybody will be okay."

"Do you really think that's what's going to happen?" Gadget asked.

Henry stood silent.

"Even if the world pays him $200 billion in gold and Dr. Stein gives him the Amulator, do you think Cobalt's going to stop the comet from striking Earth? Do you think he cares about the money? Do you think he cares about you, Maury, or anyone else in this cave?"

Henry didn't say a word. He had asked himself those same questions. He thought long and hard. It hurt to think sometimes. All he wanted to do was go home and take a nap on the couch.

"The boss says he's going to take us all with him if the world doesn't, um, pay. Isn't he?"

"Think about it," said Gadget. "Where are the spaceships to whisk you and everyone that works here to his hideout on Mars? I'll bet you that peanut butter and yogurt sandwich that there's only one spaceship on this mountain—the one that's going to take Alowishus Cobalt to safety.

"The man is mad, Henry, as mad as the hatter in *Alice in Wonderland*. He's lost all touch with reality. All he wants to do is destroy Earth. You heard him. He wants to be Master of the Universe. Every mad scientist wants to be Master of the Universe. They must have a Master of the Universe class at the mad scientist school."

Henry wanted to cry. His face wrinkled. His cheeks sagged. His hands shook.

"No, no, no. The boss says everything is, um, going to be okay. He wouldn't lie to me. He wouldn't lie to Maury, Pete, Loretta, and Eddie. Would he?"

Deep down Henry knew the truth. He knew how it would all end. He knew if Cobalt's plan succeeded, he'd never retire. He'd never see his wife again. As for building birdhouses and drinking his favorite drink— orange juice topped with whipped cream and sprinkles—he could kiss those dreams good-bye.

Henry was confused. The boss wasn't really a bad guy. He gave Henry a job when no one else would hire him. Cobalt treated him kindly, sending him birthday wishes and even a little "get well" teddy bear when Henry was sick with the flu. Cobalt protected Henry from bullies.

It was too much to think about. Henry was a sweet man, unlike most of the people who worked for Cobalt. All they wanted to do was break things. Henry just wanted to be happy. Henry bolted from the room, leaving Gadget by himself.

"Holy guacamole," Gadget muttered. "I'm doomed."

Gadget wasn't doomed, though, at least not yet. Henry bounded through the steel door five minutes later, a gust of cool air following him inside. Silent and determined, Henry took a set of keys from his pocket and unfastened the steel bracelets binding Gadget to the chair.

Gadget was free!

"You're a good man, Henry," Gadget said, bolting from the chair and rubbing his wrists. "By the way, Henry, where are we?"

Henry told him.

"Holy guacamole!"

"Here, Mr. Gadget. I think, um, you're going to need this."

Henry offered Gadget the access pad that Cobalt had stolen.

"Thanks, Henry," Gadget said. "You might just have saved the world."

"The boss is taking a nap. He's going to go, um, you know, bananas once he finds out that thingamajig is missing. You never want to see Dr. Cobalt go, you know, um, bananas. I'm fond of bananas, however, very fond of them."

Gadget nodded at Henry and pushed the access pad's "on" button, but nothing happened. "Darn," Gadget muttered. "Someone turned the power off. The access pad is useless."

"Henry, do you have a cell phone?"

Henry took a black cell phone out of his pocket. It only had one bar of service. *Maybe that will be enough*, Gadget hoped. "Cross your fingers, Henry." Gadget placed a call. The cell phone tried to connect, but the call failed.

Gadget moved to another side of the room. He closed his eyes and hit redial. This time the call went through. Gadget let out a deep breath. Colonel Bragg, his soldiers, and the Kid Squad were on their way.

"Henry, can you show me where the tractor beam is?"

Jeez Louise, Henry thought, *I hate dangerous missions*. He grudgingly nodded. "Yes, Mr. Gadget."

Chapter 9
Final Countdown

Dusk settled on Webster's Corners as the sun hid behind a patch of horsetail-like clouds. It was a beautiful early summer's night. The horizon had turned a faded shade of crimson. A gaggle of geese, all in a V-shaped formation, flew back to their nests for the day. Rising above the rolling hills was a banana-shaped new moon.

Not a soul walked down Main Street. Shop owners locked up their businesses. The town green, usually bustling with people not willing to give up a pleasant June evening, was deserted. The Shake & Stir was empty. A We're Closed sign hung from its door.

It was as if the entire town had moved somewhere else. There were only four days left before the Comet of Doom was scheduled to hit. Those who wished could see it streaking across the sky as night crept in. Ordinarily the sight of a comet is an "ooh, ahh" moment, like fireworks on the Fourth of July. Not today. Not on this night. In many ancient cultures, comets meant bad luck. And so it was again.

People, scared and unsure, huddled inside their homes. The town was eerily silent except for the howl of a dog asking to come inside. The president of the United States had told Webster's Corners and the rest of the country that the government was doing all it could to stop the comet from striking. No one believed him.

¤

At first, the sound was faint. You could barely hear it. With each passing second, however, it grew louder. *Whup-whup-whup whup-whup-whup*. It sounded like a gorilla pounding

its chest. *Whup-whup-whup, whup-whup-whup.*
Whup-whup-whup, whup-whup-whup.

The curious peeked out windows. *Whup-whup-whup, whup-whup-whup. Whup-whup-whup, whup-whup-whup.*

Nosy people, including town gossip Henrietta Soursnake, stepped out on porches and front lawns. They looked to the east. "Over there!" someone shouted, pointing at the sky. *Whup-whup-whup, whup-whup-whup. Whup-whup-whup, whup-whup-whup.*

At first, they were nothing more than tiny black dots in the fading twilight. The closer the specks came, the more noise they made. People could soon make out the shapes.

"They're helicopters," a man yelled.

He was right.

Their blades hammered against the sky. *Whup-whup-whup, whup-whup-whup. Whup-whup-whup, whup-whup-whup.*

They came in low. They came in fast. They were painted blacker than night and were sleeker than sleek. They soared by Mary-Beth Corbett's house on Oak Terrace. They shook Sam Riddle's hardware store, where a sign in the window announced "Cosmic Clearance Sale . . . Everything Must Go." Heads moved from east to west as the twenty, no, thirty, whirlybirds zoomed overhead.

"Where are they going?" someone asked.

"Looks like they're headed for the hills," someone else replied.

"With this comet coming, that's where we should be headed," another person joked. No one laughed.

In the lead helicopter sat Colonel Bragg. He looked down on Webster's Corners as his group of elite soldiers readied for battle. Each soldier was armed with a variety of weapons. Some carried the newly issued Dazer Laser that made people throw up. They called it the "Puke Ray." Others carried the Sound Hound, a high-energy cannon that used high-frequency sound waves to knock people down. Bragg's troops were ready for anything. They were always ready.

"There it is, colonel," the pilot of Bragg's helicopter said pointing. "Klondike Mountain. We'll be there in five minutes."

"It's time to open up a can of smackdown on Cobalt and his robo sentries," Bragg yelled. "Let's teach those goons a lesson."

¤

"Could you have found a smaller hole to crawl through? Sheesh!"

Athena was annoyed. She had had a hard day of walking, crawling, and stumbling. Still, D-Day had led her to an unguarded entrance on the other side of the silver mine—an old air shaft.

It was a tight squeeze—at least for Athena. Still, she was getting closer to the heart of

Cobalt's evil kingdom. Within a few minutes, D-Day and Athena were crawling through a ventilation duct above the control room.

"There's Gadget," Athena whispered, peering through an open vent. She saw Gadget and Henry through the windows of Cobalt's office. "We're almost there, D-Day." No one—not even Cobalt's ever-loyal robo sentries—paid Henry and Gadget any mind. Everyone assumed Henry was taking the prisoner to the bathroom.

Unknown to Athena, Pi and Tank were already inside the control room. Once they found out that Gadget had regained control of his access pad, Pi powered up the Amulator. She used the device to turn herself and Tank invisible. They walked through the mine's front door, right past the robo sentries. No one was the wiser. They spotted Henry and Gadget up in Cobalt's office. So they took the escalator up to the big sliding steel door. It was still open, so they let themselves in.

"The door is, um, right, right over there, Mr. Gadget, right near that picture of the boss," Henry said, standing behind Cobalt's desk. "All I have to do is, um, find the right button . . . "

Suddenly, another secret door on the opposite side of Cobalt's office slid open with a heart-thumping *whiz*. But it wasn't a door to the tractor beam room. Instead, Cobalt's shadow darkened the room.

"Henry, I am so disappointed in you," Cobalt said. "You failed me, Henry. I can't allow that to happen, no matter how many years you and I have been together. I am very, very disappointed in you."

Henry felt scolded. He wanted to say something but stopped. He felt as if he had failed his longtime friend—the guy who now wanted to destroy the world.

Cobalt walked into the room with two robo sentries. Each carried the latest edition of the Freeze Ray. The two robots pointed their weapons at Henry and Gadget and waited for the order to turn the pair into freeze-dried dog treats.

The sentries were sleek mechanical marvels. They stood seven feet high. They wore steel helmets that covered their laser-sharp eyes. They could see through walls. They could sense danger. They could fight through blistering cold and skin-peeling heat. They could run up to 100 miles an hour and were virtually indestructible.

Suddenly, alarms squealed. Bells tolled. Red lights flashed. Horns blew. Cobalt's team of robots and humans scurried like ants on a hot sidewalk. Bragg and his troops had arrived. The noise stunned Cobalt for a moment, but that's all Pi and Tank needed.

They materialized in Cobalt's office. Pi quickly zapped Cobalt with the Amulator's stun ray. Tank directed the device's rust ray at the robo sentries. Although the robots were made from an alien metal, they were no match for the Amulator. They rusted quickly. Cobalt and his now clanging pots of metal mischief fell to the floor. He was out of breath, and hopefully, Pi thought, out of time.

At that moment, Athena and D-Day lowered themselves carefully from the air duct above Cobalt's desk. The Kid Squad was back in business.

Henry wanted to do his part, too. He reached under Cobalt's desk and pushed a red button. The door to the tractor beam room, invisible to everyone, silently slid open.

Pi, Tank, Athena, Gadget, D-Day, and Henry ran into the chamber. They came face-to-face with six of Cobalt's top human thugs. They

reached for their Freeze Rays. Athena was on the ball, however. She pressed her access pad and the Amulator created a bright green beam of light. The light swept up three of Cobalt's workers and suspended them high above the floor. They were flies trapped in a spider's web.

Gadget was ready, too. He channeled the Amulator to turn the others into stone. They would stay like that for at least a day.

With the threat gone, everyone marveled at the tractor beam. It was a magnificent device only an evil scientist like Cobalt could conjure. It was cone-shaped and ten stories high. The machine was made of gleaming black, silver, and green metal.

Energy from its nuclear reactor, which was no larger than the SUV Tank's dad drove, powered this amazing monstrosity. The machine glowed with a strange greenish hue.

"Holy guacamole," Gadget muttered.

Despite all the energy coursing through its electronic veins, the device was cool to the touch. Around its base was a computerized dashboard.

On one computer screen, the kids could see an up-close image of the comet and the ion beam pulling it toward Earth. Above the screen was a digital clock that pulsated with red numbers: 1 hour, 45 minutes, 10 seconds. It was clear to all what was afoot. Cobalt had sped up the comet. Instead of four days, the raging ball of fire and ice would hit in less than two hours! Everyone gulped.

"Is there an off switch?" Tank asked.

¤

Meanwhile, in the control room and all through the old mine, Bragg's team was making quick work of Cobalt's gangsters. At first, the robo sentries put up a good fight. They had weapons no one had ever seen before. Explosion after explosion rocked Bragg's troops. No one was hurt, but a few of the unlucky had to be thawed out because of the Freeze Rays.

At the height of the battle, Bragg's troops tossed e-grenades that fried the robots' circuits and melted their computerized guts. Cobalt's human guards ran for the exits, only to surrender. Within twenty minutes, the mountain was secure.

"Where is Cobalt?" Bragg boomed to one of his captains.

"We're not sure," she said. "He should have been in the control room with those two rusted robo sentries. But he's gone. Vanished, like a puff of smoke."

It was a bit more complicated than that. When Cobalt recovered from Pi's stun ray, he crawled to an escape pod that he had built for such a moment. The pod brought him up to the top of the mountain, where a private spaceship waited. Before Bragg's troops got to his office, Cobalt was on his way to Mars. He abandoned Henry, Maury, Loretta, the whole lot of them, just as Gadget had predicted.

"Doggone it," Bragg screamed. "This is the second time he's slipped through my fingers. But he's not our main problem now. We have to disable that tractor beam. Get Dr. Stein on the double. We're going need his help."

"Yes, sir," the captain snapped. She saluted Bragg crisply and ran to fetch Dr. Stein.

Bragg bolted too, running straight to the tractor beam room. When he arrived, Dr. Stein was already there.

"Let's turn this blasted machine off now," Bragg ordered.

"It is not as easy as one would think," Dr. Stein said. "Not easy at all. Zee machine, is, how you say, booby trapped. If we try to turn it off, *kaboom*! If we try to pull the plug, *kaboom*! Everyone on zee mountain and in zee town will be *kaput*!"

"What are we going to do, Stein?" Bragg asked. "How are we going to turn this thing off?"

"Colonel Bragg," Pi said, "we can't just turn the tractor beam off. First, we have to direct the comet away from Earth."

"Zee girl is right," Dr. Stein said. "We must push zee comet back into zee original orbit."

"How do we do that?" Bragg yelled, obviously frustrated. "Let me just blast it to bits."

"Colonel, we cannot do zee blasting to bits," Dr. Stein said. "We must be careful. We must find another way."

"We need to hack into the machine," Gadget finally offered. "It has a supercomputer for a brain. We have to deceive that brain and make it do what we want it to do."

"And how do we do that, Gad?" Tank asked.

"I don't know," Gadget said.

"OMG! Will hacking into this hunk of junk blow us up?" Athena wondered.

"It might," Gadget said.

"We don't have a lot of time," Pi interrupted. "If it blows up, we won't be around to see the end of the world. If it doesn't, we might just have a chance."

Pi looked at Gadget. Gadget looked at Pi. Tank rubbed his forehead. Athena hugged D-Day.

"We will have to sync our access pads and allow the Amulator to hack into the tractor beam's brain and bypass the booby traps," Gadget said. "Once we're inside, I think I can direct the comet away from Earth using the tractor beam's controls. We can then upload a computer virus and kill the tractor beam without killing us . . . I think."

"What other choice do we have?" Pi said.

"None, as far as I can see," Henry offered. "Mr. Gadget, um, he's a smart guy. If he can't do it, then no one can."

"Okay guys, let the Amulator do its job. On my count, program your access pads. With all our access pads working at the same time, there might be just enough power to rewire this hot rod. Ready, on three. One . . . two . . . three."

Gadget programmed his access pad.

Pi did the same.

Tank looked at Athena and both did as Gadget had asked.

They waited for the Amulator to take control of the tractor beam. Would it bypass the booby traps? No one knew. Would it cause the tractor beam or its nuclear reactor to explode? It was anyone's guess.

From its secret location, the Amulator searched for an answer. It came. The lights inside the chamber went out. All the computers snapped off. The tractor beam made a high-pitched whine and began to rumble.

"It's going to explode," Athena cried. She clutched D-Day tighter.

"Give it a second." Gadget's voice cut through the darkness. Then the lights came on. The tractor beam stopped shaking. It was deathly quiet.

"We're in," Pi said. "Get to work, Gad."

Gadget sat down at the control panel. He began to type on the keyboard. It's one thing to pull a comet toward you; it's another thing to push it away. Gadget tried desperately to reverse the tractor beam. It struggled. Bragg wanted to blast a hole in the machine. Dr. Stein looked on, weary and drawn, his wire-rimmed glasses on the top of his graying head. Tank and Pi stood behind Gadget, their hands on his shoulders. D-Day clutched Athena and vice versa.

Then the entire mountain shook. It was as if they were in the middle of an earthquake. The tractor beam smoked. Sparks flew from the dashboard. One section caught fire. Rocks fell into the control room. Water pipes burst. Klondike Mountain glowed yellow and red.

"This doesn't, um, look good, Mr. Gadget," Henry said. "I'm never going to retire . . . oh, oh, Mr. Gadget . . . do something . . . do something . . . ."

¤

"C'mon Tank!" Pi cheered. "Hit a home run! All we need is a home run."

Tank dug his spikes into the dirt and took two practice swings. He always took two practice swings. The score was tied. It was the last game of the season, the last chance for Copernicus Middle School to win the ball game and the league championship.

"We're gonna lose," Athena whined. "I just know it . . . we're gonna lose."

"Shh," Dr. Stein said, his mouth brimming with a bite of a triple-decker bologna, lettuce, tomato, banana, and mustard sandwich. "Zee Tank needs to concentrate."

"I used to play ball when I was a kid," Colonel Bragg said. "I wasn't as good as Tank."

"Shh," Pi said putting her finger to her lips.

The pitcher for the other team went into his windup. He threw Tank a curve ball. The pitch caught Tank by surprise. He adjusted quickly and took a mighty swing. The ball shot off Tank's bat like a cannonball. It flew high and far.

Gadget excitedly jumped to his feet, spilling popcorn on Henry. D-Day slept under the bleachers, as quiet as a mouse. The ball cut through the air like a bullet. Copernicus Middle School fans erupted in cheers.

The ball arced over the left field fence. As the orb reached its highest point, the baseball fans of Webster's Corners saw the glowing comet in the distance. It harmlessly flew away from Earth, back to its place in the solar system.

Tank was right all along. The Kid Squad would win the ball game.